# We Lived in the Almont

### by ELEANOR CLYMER

*illustrated by David K. Stone*

E. P. DUTTON & CO., INC.  NEW YORK

The people who appear in this book do not exist
except within its covers and the mind of the author.

Published simultaneously in Canada by Clarke,
Irwin & Company Limited, Toronto and Vancouver

SBN: 0-525-39950-x (Trade) SBN: 0-525-39951-8 (DLLB)
Library of Congress Catalog Card Number: 78-116881
Designed by Hilda Scott
Printed in the U.S.A.
First Edition

*We Lived in the Almont*

*We Lived in the Almont*

# We Lived in the ALMONT

## CLYMER

ELEANOR CLYMER grew up in New York City. Although she now lives in Westchester County, she feels that city and country children are alike in many ways. She has written more than forty books for children, including *The Big Pile of Dirt* and *My Brother Stevie*. *We Lived in the Almont* once more reflects Mrs. Clymer's special ability to understand the world of the urban child.

DAVID K. STONE is a native of Oregon, now living in Port Washington, New York, with his wife and two children. He is a distinguished jacket and book illustrator of more than a hundred titles for children and adults. Mr. Stone's sensitive charcoal drawings for *We Lived in the Almont* were carefully supervised by his own thirteen-year-old daughter, Kelly.

Everybody wants something. I used to be always wanting something I couldn't have. I guess I still do. Doesn't everybody? Even grownups? I used to think grownups were different, because my mother was always telling me, You can't have everything. Be satisfied with what you have. Stop asking for the impossible.

I thought, Why does she say that? If you stop asking for the impossible, you might as well be dead. But maybe grownups get so discouraged, they just give up. Or maybe they don't like to see you disappointed. Or maybe they're afraid you'll get too mad and do something you shouldn't.

But sometimes it seems as if you can't help it. When you're young, you want things so much, you think you'll die if you can't have them.

Sometimes you don't even know what you want.

Like, when I was younger I used to mope around a lot. I was about seven, my brother Joe was twelve. He was out all the time playing in the street, and my mother would be busy with the house. She used to help Pop. He was a Super, and we always lived in these old houses, and Mama was always trying to keep the place clean. I was always complaining.

Mama would say, Linda Martin, what do you want? But I didn't really know.

So I saw this doll house in a store window, and I said I wanted that. I'd stand in front of that window and look at every single thing in that doll house, tables and chairs and beds, and the baby doll in the crib. I thought about it at night. It got so I almost couldn't sleep, I wanted it so much.

Well, I didn't get the doll house, and after a while I forgot about it and wanted something else. I wanted a pair of yellow patent shoes. This was when I was about ten. I was just crazy for those shoes. I pestered my mother for weeks. I must have been a real pain. She said she didn't have any money, but I didn't believe her. When I went to the store with her I could see she had money. I didn't understand that she didn't have enough for toys and fancy shoes. I guess I was dumb. I pestered her till finally she got disgusted and said, All right. Get them.

So we bought them and they hurt my feet. But still I liked to look at them.

Well, then when I was about twelve, I saw a picture in a magazine of a girl's room. It was so beautiful I couldn't stop looking at it. It was all white, with a white fur rug on the floor. I wanted that. Can you imagine? I showed it to Mama and said, I want a room with a fur rug.

Mama said, Linda, are you out of your mind? A fur rug! What next? Suppose you sweep the floor, that would make some sense.

She was always trying to make me help her. I hated it, because it wasn't any use. The houses we lived in were always so crummy. Old buildings with cracked plaster and lumpy paint and broken floor boards, and always roaches. You couldn't clean a place like that. All I wanted was to get out in the street and play with the kids out there. They were climbing up fire escapes and poking in trash cans and swiping things from stores. I thought they were so lucky. Mama wouldn't let me go. I guess she was right. We lived in some bad neighborhoods.

Joe was out a lot, Mama couldn't stop him, but being a girl, and younger, I had to stay in the house.

I liked school because it was a change. The teachers would praise me for doing my homework. Lots of kids couldn't even read. That didn't make the kids like me any better, so I didn't have many friends. That was something else I always wanted, some friends.

Besides, we were always moving. See, we had to live where Pop's job was, and either the building would be torn down, or it was so bad Pop couldn't fix it, and he'd find another job and we'd pack up and move. I hated moving, because it was never any better. I thought, even if the place we lived in was terrible, at least you knew what it was like. We always hoped the next place would be better and it never was.

Then finally when I was almost thirteen, we moved to the worst place of all. The worst thing about it was, our apartment was so small, only two rooms for the four of us. You couldn't ever get away from anybody. The only place was the bathroom, and that was in the hall. Maybe that's why I had this crazy idea about the room with the fur rug.

That was when Joe started staying away from home. He was seventeen. He had quit school and got a job in a garage, and Mama kept nagging him to go back to school. So he just stayed away from the house. That made it worse for me because Mama was in such a bad mood.

Well, the furnace wouldn't work, and the lights would go out, and the sinks were all stopped up. Pop couldn't fix them. And believe me, my Pop can fix anything. He should have been an engineer, only he never could go to school. Joe is the same way, that's why Mama was so upset when he quit school.

Pop got so discouraged, he would slump down in his chair when he came in for coffee. Then he and Mama would get into arguments. Mama would say, Sam, I can't take this any more. Pop would say, You don't think I like it, do you?

4

Well, one day I came in from school and they were sitting at the table and talking. They didn't even notice that I came in. Mama was saying, Sam, this is it. You'll have to do something or I'm finished.

Pop said, What can I do?

Mama said, Talk to Jim.

Jim was Pop's friend from the Army. They came from the same town. Jim used to be a plumber but he got in the real estate business and now he's real well off. He owns his home and has a big car.

Pop said, I can't go to Jim. I don't like to ask favors.

Mama said, Never mind that. It's not for yourself, it's for your family. Look at Joe. Look how he's growing up. Sam, you have to.

Pop sat there and stared at his hands, as if he didn't recognize them or something.

Finally he said, All right. And he got up and went out. A few days later he went to see Jim, and Jim knew of a job. Pop didn't think it would be much use going. He said if it was any good somebody else would have grabbed it. But Mama kept talking to him, and finally he went there, and what do you know, he got the job.

He came back looking real pleased. He brought some beer and sat down and drank it. Mama asked him what the place was like, but he wouldn't tell her. He went there every day for a week to get it ready. Finally he borrowed a truck and he and Joe loaded our things in it, the beds and chairs and a couple of trunks, and we rode downtown.

It was Sunday. It was a nice sunny day in summer,

and we rode past some real nice streets and houses, not slums like we had been living in. People were out walking with their good clothes on. Pop was in a good mood. I don't know when I ever saw him so happy.

Finally he stopped the truck in front of a building and said, All off.

Mama said, What do you mean, all off?

He said, I mean this is it.

Mama sat there looking at the building. She said, Sam! You mean it? And he said, Yes.

Mama was speechless. She just stared. Finally she said, It's beautiful!

I thought so too. I could hardly believe it. It wasn't like any other house we had ever lived in. It had a big front stoop with two stone lions, one on each side. The lions' noses and tails were a little bit broken, but we didn't notice it then. There was a big front door with colored glass in the top. And over the door was the name, ALMONT, carved in the stone.

Mama explained to us later, that that's how they used to make the best buildings in the old days, where rich people lived. And this used to be a very good building. Now it wasn't so swell any more, and nobody in it was rich. I didn't know that at the time. I saw some people leaning out of their windows, looking down at us, and I thought, Those must be rich people living here.

Pop said, Well, you just want to sit here, or should we go inside? So we went in, and then we stared some more. The hallway was wide, with a marble floor and a big wide staircase. Of course the floor had cracks, and

the stair rail had some parts missing, but who cared about that? It was big and light, not dark and narrow like that other place.

We went on back and Pop unlocked a door, and showed us our apartment. Well, I'll never forget that first look. The rooms were so light! I'll never forget those empty rooms with the sun shining through the dusty windows.

Mama kept saying, My goodness! My goodness! Sam, are you sure you didn't make a mistake? And Pop just grinned at her.

There was a living room with a dining room attached to it, and a big kitchen and two bedrooms. One of the bedrooms was small. Mama said Joe should have it. I could see she was hoping he'd stay home more. But Joe said no, he didn't need it, he'd sleep in the dining room. But then we found another room, a tiny little room off the kitchen.

Mama said it was the maid's room. I said, Are we going to have a maid? Mama laughed and said that in the old days each family had a maid, and this was where she slept, so she could get up early and cook breakfast. Mama said, You can be the maid. So that was how I got my own room.

Joe and Pop brought in our furniture. We didn't have much, and Mama said, We will start saving up for a sofa. Then there was a surprise. Pop and Joe went away and soon they came back with another man helping them, and they were bringing a sofa!

Mama screamed, Where did you get that?

Pop said some tenant had left it in the basement, and he found it and fixed the springs. Mama almost cried. Then she laughed. Then she said, All right, we'll start saving for a rug. All my life I wanted a sofa and a rug.

I was surprised when I heard that. It was the first time I ever thought about her wanting something like that.

Then Pop had to take the truck back, and Joe helped us put up the beds. Then Mama sent me to the store to get stuff for supper. The store was around the corner. There were some ladies there, talking. When I walked in they looked at me and one said, Aren't you the new Super's girl? I said yes, and she said, That's nice. Tell your father I'd like to see him in 5B.

I got the groceries and the man winked at me and gave me a candy bar. I went home and told Mama about the ladies, and she said, I suppose they're thinking up jobs for him already. Well, they'll get good service. It's about time he had a decent job, a man like him!

We washed the dishes, and Pop came back and ate supper, and I went outside on the stoop and leaned on one of the lions. I watched the street lights go on, and the sun go down at the end of the street, and I thought, This is a good place. I have my own room, and Pop has a good job, and Joe is home. It's going to be different now.

For the first time since I could remember, I couldn't think of anything to wish for.

We all felt good. Pop liked the job. Mama was in a good mood and didn't nag Joe so much. She started fixing the house. The very first day after we moved in, after Pop drank his coffee and went out, Mama said to me, Now we are going to get this place clean and I mean *clean*.

She started cleaning the kitchen. Boy did she scrape grease off the stove! I scrubbed the bathroom. I even enjoyed it. I scrubbed the tub and the sink and polished the faucets. They were brass—all the chrome had worn off—and when you polished them they looked like gold. I scrubbed the tiles and there was a design on them of little blue flowers, under the dirt.

We had a good time working together, because it was worth while. When we got through it looked like something. Mama washed the floors and waxed them. She said we didn't really need a rug because the floors were so nice. They were made of little pieces of wood fitted together. Mama said she once worked in a house where they had floors like that, called parquet.

The living room had a mantel piece made of wood carved in a fancy design, with a mirror over it. We washed the mirror, and the windows, and Mama said we would make curtains, and we would get paint and paint the rooms. She looked in the trunk where she kept things, and took out two pictures in gold frames. They were of my grandfather and grandmother. I remembered seeing them when I was little, but I didn't know she still had them. We hung them over the sofa.

Mama said, How do they look?

I said they looked fine, and she said, I always wanted a nice room where I could hang them up. Those other houses, there never was a place for them.

Then she said, We must fix up your room. But I don't know where we can get a fur rug. (She was teasing me. That meant she was feeling good.) She looked in the trunk again and found an old bedspread for me, and Pop got me a bureau that somebody left in the basement. And we fixed the dining room. Mama bought a table in a second-hand store. Of course we didn't do all this in one day.

We'd work, and then it would be lunch time and Pop would come in for lunch, all dirty because he was working on the furnace. He said it needed fixing all

11

right, but he thought he could do it by the time cold weather came. He talked about the things he was going to do, paint the halls and fix the bannister and that. He said, When I get through you'll be proud of this place. There won't be any complaints.

Mama said, That's all right but I never saw a tenant yet that didn't complain. They don't appreciate what you do for them.

Pop said, Oh, no, these are nice people. I think this time we really have it made.

Just then there was a knock at the door and when I went to open it there was a woman with a cake in her hand.

She said, I'm Mrs. Lopez from 5A and I brought this to say hello to the new Super.

I could see Mama was so surprised she didn't know what to do. She said, Well thanks but you didn't need to.

But the woman said, I know how it feels to be in a new place, and I want you to know we're glad to have you here. It's a nice house, I've been here two years and I have seven kids, all nice kids.

Then she looked at me and said, I got a girl your age, you can be friends.

Then she went away, but just as she was going she said, Oh, by the way that Mrs. Ferguson in 4A is always complaining, don't pay any attention to her, she's a nervous woman.

Then she left. Pop laughed and said he knew Mrs.

Ferguson, she lived right underneath the seven kids and she was nervous all right.

We ate the cake and it was real good. All the time I was eating it I thought, Gee, I'd like to meet that lady's daughter. The lady is nice, maybe her kids will be nice too.

I met her that afternoon. I was going to the store and she was standing on the stoop with some boys. They were laughing and fooling, and when I came out they stopped.

I was embarrassed, because I wasn't too good at talking to boys, even if I did have a brother. Joe's friends were all older and they didn't pay much attention to me.

This girl said, Hi, I'm Carol Lopez. We live in 5A.

I said, I'm Linda Martin. We just moved here.

She said, Yes, I know, we watched you moving in. We were looking out the window. My mother was down to your house today. This is my brother Vince, and this is Freddie Keating. He lives in 5B, he's got two brothers.

I said Hi to them.

Carol said, I'm glad there's another girl in the house, there's too many boys already, ha, ha.

I said I was going to the store, and she said, After you're through come out and we'll talk.

When I came back, the boys were gone, so Carol asked me up to her apartment. The apartment was just like ours, but it was so full of furniture you could

hardly move. Lots of upholstered chairs, and shiny wood tables, and mirrors, and pictures on the walls of weddings and graduations, and beds everywhere. I thought, My, it would take us years to get as much furniture as that.

We went into Carol's room that she shared with her two sisters, and she showed me her things, sweaters and bras, and some cigarettes that she kept hidden in case her mother or her little sister found them. She asked me all about my brother, how old he was and what he did. She said she saw him going out to work and he was cute. She sure did like boys.

I was a little embarrassed when she talked about them all the time. Still, I liked her and was glad to have a friend. She took me all over and I got to know the neighborhood. It was different from where we lived before. That was all one kind of house. But here, along the park, were these big new apartment houses where rich people lived. And in the side streets were some old brownstone buildings that were mostly rooming houses. There were a few old tenements full of poor people, and then there was the Almont. It was mixed.

Well, pretty soon school started, and Carol and I went together. We were in some of the same classes.

The school was okay. I liked my teachers, much better than in that other school where we had to sit two in a seat and the teacher did nothing but yell at us. This wasn't a new school but it was nice, with lots of room, and plants in the windows. And I was doing pretty good work, but it wasn't so easy as in my other school, because most of the kids were pretty smart. It was fun being with smart kids, you had to be on your toes or you'd get left behind, and if the teacher gave us a hard problem and you got the answer fast, the others didn't give you dirty looks—they looked as if they were thinking, Hey, pretty good!

So I am happy. I thought, For once things are great. And then I began to want something else.

See, now we had this nice apartment, Joe was home more. Mama wanted him to go to school, but he said he would have to go in the Army so why bother. Mama didn't like that, but she stopped nagging at him, in fact I overheard Pop talking to her and saying something about leaving Joe alone and maybe he would be easier to live with.

And he was. He'd tease Mama—he liked to come home in his dirty clothes and start to sit down on the sofa, and Mama would scream, Don't you dare sit down!

Then he'd laugh and say, I just wanted to make you yell.

And he'd help me with my homework, and tell about some of the customers at the garage.

And now that we had a big apartment he even brought his friends around. They would sit in the front room and drink cokes or beer. They'd watch baseball, and sometimes they would sing. There was one friend of Joe's named Dave. He had a guitar. He had a nice voice and when he played and sang it made shivers go down my back. I almost loved him when he played. Actually he was pretty ugly. He had pimples and dandruff. But when he was playing you forgot that.

He'd see me watching him and say, Come here, kid. You want to try this here guitar?

And he'd show me how to tune it and play the chords. It was fun. I started wishing I had one of my own. Of course I didn't know how I'd ever get one.

But then Dave had to go away somewhere, to Army camp or someplace for a couple of weeks, and he left his guitar at our house. He said to me, You keep it for me, kid.

I asked him, Should I play it?

He said, Sure, you play it and keep it in tune. That's the best way to take care of it. You do that.

So after that, every chance I had, I played the guitar. I'd listen to music on TV and pick out the tunes. I'd sit on my bed and play by the hour. I missed Dave. I'd think about him and forget all about his pimples, and imagine what he'd say when he came back and heard me play.

My mother would call me to eat, or go to the store, and I hardly heard her. Of course I had to stop sometimes. Mama said it was driving her crazy.

Then Dave came back. But not to stay. He had a girl, and was going to get married and go away. Joe had a party for him. I never even got a chance to show Dave how I could play. After the party he took back the guitar, and he and his girl left. Well, of course he *was* older than me. But I was sick about it, and kept dreaming about him and the guitar.

There was a store I passed on the way to school, where they sold records and guitars and band instruments. I saw a guitar in the window, dark wood with mother of pearl on top, and I went in and asked the man how much it was. I thought maybe I could earn money and save up for it. The man asked me if I wanted to buy it.

I said, No, my family wants to get one for my brother and we have to save up, but I'd like to know.

He said it was $200. Well, I might as well have wanted a fur coat and a car. I thought, I'll have to grow up and earn money, but first I'll have to get through school, and then learn to be a secretary. I'll be in school the rest of my life probably.

Then something happened that made me forget about the guitar.

It was a Sunday. Carol was away, visiting her aunt, and was it quiet! In our old neighborhood there was plenty going on, even if it was only people hitting each other. But here, on our block at least, it was quiet, with church bells ringing and people all dressed up for church, or ladies in pants from the swell buildings taking their dogs out.

Well, this Sunday I was standing out front wishing I had something to do. Joe was out, and Mama and Pop were inside taking a nap. It was getting to be fall, sort of cool and nippy. The air smelled good, an exciting kind of weather. You feel like doing something but you don't know what.

I was just thinking I'd go to the park, when somebody said, Hi. There was this girl I knew from school. Her name was Sharon Ross. She was in my English and math classes.

I said Hi to her and thought she was going by, but she stopped and said, Is this where you live?

I said yes, and she said, Oh, I didn't know that. Why, we're practically neighbors.

She said she lived just around the corner, so I knew she meant in one of the buildings near the park. She asked me what I was doing.

I said, Nothing, and she said, Me too. I should be doing my homework, but it's such nice weather. My whole family went out, so I thought I'd go out for a while. Want to go to the park?

I said, Sure, wait till I tell my mother.

I went inside and said, Mama, I'm going for a walk with a girl I know.

She said, That's nice, dear, and closed her eyes again.

We went to the park and Sharon said, Let's go to the swings.

I thought, Does she mean the baby playground? That sounds crazy. But that's what she meant.

She said, I love to swing, but I feel like a fool going by myself.

So we grabbed a couple of swings and started to

pump. I hadn't been on a swing since I was about three, and I'd forgotten how much fun it was. We raced each other, and laughed like anything. Then we got off so some little kids could have a turn, and we went on the seesaw.

Then Sharon said, I'm hot, let's get some ice cream. She had some money in her pants pocket. I forgot to say she was wearing jeans and a turtle neck sweater. I felt awfully dressed up in my dress and coat which I had put on because it was Sunday.

We found an ice cream man and sat on a bench and ate. We watched the people go past. There were old ladies feeding pigeons, and couples with their arms around each other, and people with dogs. There was a fat lady with a tiny little dog, and a skinny lady with a great Dane, and we laughed at them all. I hadn't had so much fun in years.

We talked about everything, about school, and where we were born, and stuff like that. Would you believe it, we were almost twins. I was a week older. Sharon had an older sister and I had an older brother.

Then we talked about our parents. Sharon said her father was a lawyer. What does your father do? she asked me.

I didn't answer for a second. Then I said, He's the Super in our house. Then I waited to see what she would say.

She said, No kidding! That means you can play any-where you like! You're lucky.

I said, You think so?

She said, Well, everywhere I ever lived, you'd start to play and somebody would say, Look out the Super's coming, and we'd have to quit.

I could see she had her own idea of what a Super does.

It was starting to get twilight, it was chilly, and the sky was greenish blue, and the park lights went on. I heard the church clock bong five times, and I said, I've got to go.

Sharon said, Me too. And I haven't done my math. I hate it.

I said, I could help you with it.

She said, Could you? You mean it?

Sure, I said. Come to school early tomorrow.

So we walked home and said, See you tomorrow.

I went in, and Mama was fixing supper. She said, What's the idea of staying out so late? Where were you?

I said, Oh, just having fun. And I turned on the radio. I felt like dancing.

I COULD hardly wait to get to school the next day. I wondered if Sharon would be there, and she was. She was waiting for me in the yard with her math book open.

She said, Come on, hurry up, you promised to help me.

I explained the problems, they were really easy, but she sighed and said she'd never understand them.

It was phys-ed day and we were both wearing white blouses and blue skirts. I can still remember there was something special about her clothes. They didn't seem any different from mine but they seemed to fit better. They even smelled nice. She always had that nice smell. I used to wonder what it was—not perfume but sort of fresh, like some kind of soap.

Finally the bell rang and we went in. Sharon wasn't so good in math—she got three wrong out of six—but she sure was good in gym. She could climb up a rope or turn a double somersault or a cartwheel like nothing at all. And basketball! She never missed a basket. I felt clumsy alongside her.

After school we walked home together. We got to my house and I was just saying, See you tomorrow, when Sharon said, What are you doing this afternoon?

I said, Nothing. And she said, I'll just go home and change my clothes and be right back.

So in a few minutes she was back with her jeans on. I introduced her to Mama, and Mama said, I'm glad to know you, do you live around here?

When she told Mama the building she lived in, Mama knew right away. She nodded and said, Oh!

Then she gave us some cake and milk. Sharon said, Boy, this is good cake. Did you make it, Mrs. Martin? Mama said yes, and Sharon said, I wish my mother knew how to make cake.

I changed my clothes and we went out. Sharon said, Look! No elevator! Let's go up.

We went up all five flights of stairs and out on the roof. The wind was blowing out there and we leaned against it, and watched the pigeons flying around, and the smoke from the chimneys. Far off we could see the river with boats on it.

Sharon said, Some time I'm going to have a boat. I'll be the captain and we'll sail around the world.

I said, How can a girl be a captain?

She said, A girl can be anything. Why not? Maybe I'll be a mountain climber.

She told me that last summer she had gone mountain climbing with her father. She said, I love to be up high. My father is a good mountain man. He climbed the Alps when he was in college. But my mother doesn't like it too much. She'd rather swim or play tennis. Do you play tennis?

I was wondering what it would be like to have your father climb mountains. My father just climbed stairs. But I didn't say that. I just said, No, I never did. You need a tennis racket.

She said, I tell you what. We could borrow one of my mother's rackets and go to the park and play. You could get a permit.

Jeepers! I never thought of doing that.

I said, Well, I don't know how.

Oh, you'd pick it up, she said. I'll teach you. Come on, let's go over to my house now.

I said, It's late now. I have to help my mother.

So we decided to go the next day. I told Mama where we were going and she looked as if she wasn't sure she wanted me to go. We went around the corner into the building. It was a great big new building with two towers with gold on top. It had two elevators. The doorman opened the door for us, and we went up in the elevator about twenty floors. My ears felt funny.

Sharon said, Swallow, just like you do in a plane.

I thought, Plane! Who goes in planes? Then I figured, She does.

We went into the apartment and I thought, Wow!

All across the front of the living room was glass. You could stand there and look down and see the whole park. I had to grab hold of a chair, I felt almost as if I was going to fall out.

Sharon said, Come in Mother's room, I'll see if I can find a racket.

I said, Will she mind?

She said, Oh, no. Anyhow she isn't home. She's working.

I asked, Where does she work? And Sharon said, Oh, she's in her studio. She paints.

I had noticed there were pictures all over the walls. Those are some of her pictures, Sharon told me.

I thought, Imagine having a mother who paints pictures and plays tennis.

We found the racket and some balls and went down. Sharon said we couldn't go to the park till I got a permit.

I asked her, How do you get a permit? And she said, Oh, you go to the Parks Department and pay three dollars. I'll go with you.

I thought, Three dollars! Where will I get three dollars?

Sharon said we'd find a place to practice, some place where there was a wall. Then I remembered. In the Almont, in back, there was a wall without any win-

dows. Maybe Pop would let us play there. So we went back to my house and down in the basement and found Pop. I couldn't find him at first, so I called, and he came out of a dark corner with a wrench in his hand.

He said, Oh, what are you doing here? Does somebody want me? I got a leak in a pipe, I can't go now.

I said, No, nothing is the matter. Pop, this is Sharon, and we want to play tennis. Can we go out in the back yard?

He said okay, and unlocked the back door for us.

Sharon looked around and said, This is a great place!

It was a nice big yard, and Pop had cleaned it up. It used to have a lot of junk and bottles that people threw down, but now there was nothing except some old washtubs that he was going to get rid of.

Sharon showed me how to bat the ball against the wall, and then bat it back when it came at me. She could keep it up for half an hour if she wanted. It looked easy, but just try and get to where the ball bounced in time to hit it! But after a while I started to get the idea. It was fun.

We played till we got tired. Then we sat down on a couple of washtubs and rested.

Sharon talked about the trips she and her father took. She said he always wanted to be an explorer but he couldn't afford it, so he became a lawyer. So on his vacations he took these trips to wild places. He had been to Africa and brought back a lot of carvings. I remembered then I had seen some peculiar looking

27

things on the bookshelves in her apartment—animals
and masks and that.

Sharon looked at her watch and said she had to go
home. We went in through the basement. It was dark
and mysterious in there, with pipes overhead and old
refrigerators standing around like big white ghosts.

Sharon laughed. It's great down here, she said. You
could play hide and seek. It would be great.

We went into our apartment and Mama gave us
doughnuts and milk. Then Sharon said, More math tomorrow. Will you help me again?

I said I would. I was glad I could help her with something, even if it was only math. Then she went home.

I asked Mama if I could get a permit to play tennis
in the park.

Mama said, Permit? That costs money, doesn't it?

I said, Yes. Three dollars.

Mama said, Where am I going to get three dollars?
And then you need a racket.

She said I could use her mother's racket, I said.

Joe came in then and said, What's all this about?

So I told him and he said, Oh, come on, Mom, the
kid ought to have some fun. I'll give her the three
dollars.

So the next afternoon Sharon and I went to the park
and I got my permit. After that we played almost every
afternoon. Sharon showed me how. The idea was to
smash that ball with the racket as hard as you could.
Only she could always smash harder than me. Once in
a while I would win a game, but mostly she won. I

didn't mind. The only thing I did mind was, I wished I had some white shorts and a big thick sweater like hers. Only I didn't want to ask Mama for the money. So I wore my gym shorts.

Well, it got colder, and we had to quit playing tennis. One Saturday we went on a hike.

Sharon had a knapsack that she got from her father, and took some stuff for lunch. We walked along the river till we came to a place where we could make a fire. We cooked some hot dogs and made melted cheese sandwiches, and drank cocoa out of a thermos bottle.

Boy, was that good! And the whole entire time we never stopped talking.

She told me about her family. She had a whole lot of uncles and aunts and a grandmother in this place they came from, in Massachusetts. Sometimes she had to go there for a family reunion, and did she hate it! She had to wear dresses all the time, and white gloves, and they expected her to act like a lady. She had to go to church on Sunday and wear a hat and keep quiet. But after church she used to sneak out and climb trees with the boys and go swimming in the brook.

One time the boys dared her to go swimming without anything on, so they all did, and her grandmother found out and raised a fuss. Her grandmother had a horse for her to ride, and after that she wasn't allowed to ride for a week. I think she liked the horse better than anybody there.

It sounded like something from another world. I

tried to picture what it was like, but I couldn't.

I wanted to tell about my family, but I couldn't seem to make them sound interesting. Anything I said about them just sounded sort of gloomy, like my father coming here because he wanted to go to school and be an engineer, only he couldn't, and had to be a Super instead. And my mother too, she wanted to be a teacher, but she had to go to work instead, to help her family.

At last we put out the fire and walked home. It was getting dark, and the wind was cold, and the lights were on in the houses. We leaned over the railing and watched the cars on the road by the river, with their lights shining as they flew along. We looked up and saw a plane overhead, its red and green lights winking.

We walked into the house, our faces all red from the cold, and it was nice and warm there. My mother was in the kitchen fixing supper.

She said, For goodness sake, where were you? I almost called the police.

Sharon laughed and said, My, that smells good!

So Mama said, You want to stay for supper? Call up your mother and ask her. But Sharon had to go home because her aunt was coming.

Later on I thought of something I forgot to tell her, and called her on the phone.

My mother said, For heaven sake, didn't you just see her? Didn't you say everything you had to say?

But it seemed as if we never said everything we had to say. There was always something more.

## 4

AFTER I met Sharon, I didn't go with Carol so much. She'd walk to school with us, but we didn't have too much to say, and after school she generally had to pick up her little sister at *her* school. We could have gone with her, but we didn't. I felt mean because she was really a good kid.

Sharon had some friends who lived in some of the buildings near hers. Their parents were friends of her parents. They used to come up to Sharon's house sometimes and play records, and talk about sailing, or horseback riding, or what their big sisters did on dates. Most of them went to private school. One girl asked Sharon once why she didn't go to private school. Sharon said her mother believed in public school. I never could think of anything to say to them.

Really I just wanted to be with Sharon. I liked it at her house. Once in a while her mother was home. Her mother was just beautiful. She was thin and dark, and had smooth shiny hair, and wore wild clothes, all colors. I wished my mother would fix herself up a little.

Mrs. Ross asked me what I wanted to be. She said it was important to know. One time I had a poem in the class paper and she said I had talent.

But mostly I liked to look at their house. It was so beautiful. The furniture was plain dark wood, all polished but dull, not shiny. And the sofas were so soft, you felt as if you were sitting on a cloud. They were covered with velvet, or some kind of woven stuff, all different colors. In the middle of the dining room table would be just one big bowl. And in a corner, standing on the floor, just a big white jar with a dead branch in it. You would never think that could look so beautiful.

When I went home and looked at our house, I would get very dissatisfied. I'd think, Mama can fix this place till kingdom come and it'll never look like anything. I forgot how nice the Almont looked when I first saw it.

And once when I was up in Carol's house, I remembered that day I first saw it, and I wondered how I could ever have liked all those mirrors and shiny stuff and overstuffed chairs.

I guess I acted pretty terrible sometimes, especially if Sharon had to go somewhere else, or if I had to stay home on account of my mother's relatives coming. Sometimes Mama would get mad and say, Linda, I don't

32

know what has come over you. When we first moved here you were such a help to me. Now you act as if we're not good enough for you.

I said, I do not. But I guess it was true.

Sharon never acted like that. She liked to come to our house. She said, It's so nice, your mother is always home.

Once I had dinner at her house. I noticed everything they had, the silver and place mats and glasses, all put on the table like a picture in a magazine. I tried to remember how it looked, the way I used to remember that doll house. Sharon was helping her mother set the table, and her mother said, Sharon, turn the knife blades in, and put the salad forks on the inside.

I thought, Imagine your mother telling you to turn the knife blades in!

After dinner her family was going out, so we were going to do our homework together. Then Sharon got the idea I should sleep there. Her mother said, Why not? You could keep Sharon company. Phone your mother and ask if it's all right.

Mama said, No, you better come home. But then Mrs. Ross got on the phone and said it would be doing her a favor so Sharon shouldn't be alone. So Mama agreed. She said I should come home and get my pajamas, but Mrs. Ross said Sharon could lend me some, and even an extra toothbrush. So I stayed.

After her parents and her sister went out, I thought

we should wash the dishes, but Sharon just put them in the dishwasher. She scraped the plates in the sink, and crash! she dropped one.

Oh, shucks, she said, it's one of the good plates. Mother will have a fit. Then she dropped a glass.

She laughed. I'm really clumsy tonight, she said. We better get out of here. She turned a knob, and the water started running inside the dishwasher, and in about a half hour it all stopped, and that was it. We didn't bother to do the pots or the roasting pan.

Sharon said, Selena will do them in the morning. You know what? Let's look at my sister's guitar. She just got it for her birthday.

We went in her sister's room. It was a pretty room, with a pink rug and a pink and white spread and white embroidered curtains and a dressing table with white embroidery around the bottom. I said, Gee, this is pretty.

Sharon said, Oh, do you like it? I can't stand it.

Then I remembered, her room had brown and orange corduroy cushions and couch covers, and some of those African masks on the walls, and a big sign that said PEACE NOW.

She took the guitar out of the case, and said, I'm not allowed to touch it. If Betsy knew, she'd have a fit. She thinks I'm clumsy.

It's true she was clumsy about handling things. It was funny, she was so good at anything athletic. She started plunking the guitar.

34

I said, Can I try it? L 1557985

I tuned it the way Dave had showed me, and played some chords and we sang a few songs.

We forgot all about homework, we were having so much fun. Sharon said, I wish I had a guitar, but Mother says I have to play the piano. She won't get me a guitar. She says I have too much stuff already.

Finally about ten o'clock I was getting pretty sleepy, and I said, Maybe we should do some homework. But Sharon said she wanted to try the guitar. But before she could touch it we heard a key in the lock, and Sharon yelled, Yikes! That must be Betsy. I didn't know she was coming home so early.

We jammed the guitar back in the case and stuck it in Betsy's room, and rushed through the bathroom into Sharon's room. We were sitting there trying not to laugh, but nearly exploding.

Then we heard Betsy call, Sharon, are you there?

Sharon squeaked, Yes, we're doing our homework.

Betsy went in her room, and Sharon whispered, She's looking to see if we were in there.

Pretty soon Betsy came in and looked at us and said, Sharon, did you touch my guitar?

Sharon looked awfully guilty, so I said, Well, actually I did. I saw the case and asked Sharon if I could see it.

Sharon said, Linda knows how to play, she's real good.

Betsy didn't say any more, because I was company,

but I was betting that as soon as I was gone she would let Sharon have it, and lock up the guitar when she went out.

We decided to go to bed then, and get up real early and do our homework in the morning. So we took our showers and Sharon lent me some pajamas, and a bathrobe to match, and we got in bed. She had twin beds in her room in case she had company. The sheets were as smooth as silk, it was nice to just move my feet around between them.

Sharon wanted to talk, but I fell asleep, and the next thing I knew, it was morning and we had to hurry. I had to stop off home and get a clean blouse, and when I walked in the Almont I could hardly bear it, it looked so beat up and old. My Pop was in the hall mopping the floor. I said, Hi, Pop, but I was thinking, Why does he have to do that? When I left Sharon's house, her father was all dressed up in a suit and tie, drinking coffee and reading the paper. It was like seeing my Pop for the first time.

I went in the apartment and Mama was in the kitchen. She had a pile of laundry on the floor, ready to go to the launderette, and the dirty dishes were in the sink. I thought, Why can't she have a kitchen like Sharon's mother's?

Then I went and got a clean blouse—there were three of them in the closet, and I thought that Mom must have ironed last night, because I only had one clean one left yesterday.

She said, Did you have a good time? I said, Yes, it was nice over there but I have to go to school now. G'by.

And I rushed out. I ran to school and got there just in time. It was the first time I ever went to school without doing any homework at all, and it sure was an awful feeling. I kept wishing the day would end before I got called on, but it didn't. I had to make a few guesses in Spanish and math, and we had a quiz in English. I wrote a lot of stuff I didn't know anything about.

When I got my paper back the teacher had written on it, Not your usual style, Linda.

Boy did I feel stupid.

Well, after that I was sort of torn between two different lives. I looked at everything in our house and thought how crummy it looked. I knew it wasn't nice to think that way but I couldn't help it.

One time Sharon said, You know what? My folks are going to be away overnight and I could sleep at your house if you want.

Well, I didn't know what to do. I said, I'll ask Mama. Then I went home and said to Mama, Can Sharon sleep over Friday night?

Mama said, Well, I guess so, but where will she sleep?

I wished I had a big room with twin beds in it, but I didn't. I said, She can have my room and I'll sleep on the couch. Mama said okay.

So I rushed home from school to help Mama clean.

I cleaned my room and put clean sheets on the bed. I said, Haven't we got any decent sheets? Then I remembered towels. In Sharon's bathroom each person had their own color towels and wash cloths. Sharon's was yellow and her sister's was pink, and I mean thick towels like you see in *Life* magazine. When I stayed there she said, The blue towels are yours.

So I looked for some towels, but ours were all thin and worn out and none of them matched except two that my aunt sent for a present when we moved in, but they were dirty.

I said, Can I wash these towels Aunt Ida sent? And Mama said, What are you making so much fuss about, you'd think Mrs. Rockefeller was coming.

I didn't answer but I was hoping Joe would remember to use his own towel and not wipe his dirty hands on Sharon's.

Well, as usual Sharon didn't mind anything, the only thing was that when we were doing the dishes after supper, I was washing and she was drying, she kept saying, This tea towel is wet, where can I find another one? Then she'd hand me back the forks because they weren't clean enough. I couldn't get them any cleaner, that's the way they were. I finally said, We'll just let them soak.

When it was time to go to bed I thought, I hope she remembered to bring pajamas because the only ones I can lend her have the buttons off. Mama told me to sew them on but I forgot. Well, fortunately she did bring hers, and she got in my bed and I sat on the end and we talked till Mama yelled at us to go to sleep.

I woke up real early and hurried to clean up the living room and fold my blankets so it would look nice when Sharon got up.

WELL, Sharon never noticed things like that, or if she did, she didn't care. But I did. And the thing I noticed the most was, the more I tried to make everything look nice and do everything right, the more impossible it was. Sometimes I'd forget, and look at the Almont the way it looked the day I first saw it, when I was comparing it to that place we came from. But mostly it looked hopeless and the people all looked grubby. So I made believe I thought it was funny. I don't remember just how that started, I guess I just wanted to make Sharon laugh. She had a real loud laugh that I liked to hear.

One time Sharon was telling about visiting her grandmother and going sailing and riding that horse. I thought to myself, heck, while she was horseback riding

I was taking the clothes to the launderette, or listening to some tenant complaining that the hot water was cold, or there were too many roaches.

And while Mr. Ross would be climbing a mountain, my father would be down in the basement trying to fix some old pipe. I remembered once he came up from the basement and was telling Mama that he was on his back under some pipes, and a rat came out and sat there and looked at him, and he couldn't get up, but grabbed his wrench and threw it at the rat, and it hit the cement floor and broke. Of course he missed the rat. (This happened in the other building. We didn't have any rats in the Almont.)

My brother started to laugh at Pop breaking the wrench on account of a rat, and Pop got so mad at Joe he grabbed a coffee cup and almost threw it at Joe, but he dropped it on the floor instead. Then Mama gave it to him for breaking her good cup.

I told Sharon about it, and she laughed like crazy, we both laughed so hard we almost got a stomach ache. So I got in the habit of telling her that kind of story. It seemed that if I couldn't tell her about nice things, I'd tell about the crummiest things I could think of.

I'd tell about the tenants. Some of them were pretty funny. Like, there was this woman with red hair in 4B. When she was going out she would get all dressed up as if she was going to Mrs. Rockefeller's house, and she'd walk down the stairs not looking at anybody, as if nobody was good enough for her.

Then there was this skinny old lady on the same floor, in 4A, her name was Mrs. Ferguson. She had lived in the building since the year one. She was always talking about the way things used to be when her husband was alive. He used to be a missionary in China. The way she talked he was some kind of a saint. Every time the red-headed lady went down the stairs, she would stick her head out and say, Hmf! Riff-raff!

One time Mrs. Ferguson put an old chair out in the hall for the Salvation Army to take. But when the Salvation Army came, the chair wasn't there. Mrs. Ferguson said, Hmf! Riff-raff took it.

Mama thought she was just being mean, but Pop said that one day when he had to go to the red-headed lady's apartment to fix something, there was the chair. He said her hair wasn't red when she was home.

Then there was this Mrs. Keating who lived on the same floor as the Lopezes. She had a married daughter with a baby, and three sons, the youngest was Freddie. The daughter used to come with the baby and cry, and then her husband would come and take her back. Mrs. Keating told Mama the husband drank and wasn't good enough for her daughter. She was always bragging about her two older boys, but she had trouble with Freddie. He played hooky a lot. Pop found him in the basement a couple of times fooling around his workbench. Pop said, What do you want? And Freddie said he'd like to make something with tools. So Pop showed him how, and he made a box and gave it to Carol. He sure liked Carol. Pop said the kid was really good with tools and it was too bad he didn't get some training. Pop gave him a couple of tools. He liked Pop a lot.

Then there was this couple, a man and a woman, Mr. and Mrs. Berger. The wife went to work but the husband was retired and he had nothing to do but sit in the front window and watch whoever went in and out, and if anything happened, he would report it.

Once he saw a man going along the street trying all the car doors, and called the police. But by the time they came the man was gone. And one time he saw a man going out the door with an armful of clothes. He ran after him and said, Where are you going with those things?

The man said, To the cleaner, and you better mind your own business or you'll be sorry. It turned out it was a man who lived in the building. There was this woman, Mrs. Quinn, who rented out all her rooms except the maid's room, where she slept with her dog, and this was one of her roomers. But Pop said that with Mr. Berger it was as good as having a cop in the house.

There was a girl who was crippled or something, she was in a wheel chair and couldn't talk well, her hands were always shaking. She was about eighteen and had never gone to school. Of course there was nothing funny about that, it was very sad because they said she was very smart and should have gone to a special school somewhere. We felt sorry for her, and sometimes we'd bring her magazines or get her books from the library.

She liked to talk to us and I guess she was pretty lonesome. I wish now we'd gone to see her more often. Her father worked at night and her mother worked in the daytime so somebody could be home with her.

But the funniest one was this woman who lived in 1A, right in front. Her name was Miss Clark. We used to call her the Plant Lady. She was crazy for plants. Her apartment was full of them. She had so many they were even climbing up the windows. She didn't have any curtains. In the daytime you couldn't see through the windows, but at night, if you stood on the sidewalk, you could see the light shining through the leaves, and she'd be sitting inside with a cat on her lap, typing on a typewriter. It sure looked weird.

The other tenants were always talking about Miss Clark. They said she wasn't right in her head, and people like that could go crazy and do things. Mrs. Ferguson said it wasn't sanitary having all those plants in the house, because they brought bugs, and Pop should call the Housing or the Health Department and have them do something.

Sharon and I and the other kids used to watch the Plant Lady. We'd see her go out sometimes with a big box. She'd come back with it full of old plants. We followed her once and she went to the park and brought home the ones the men pulled out and threw away.

She used to wear an old gray sweater and sneakers, with her gray hair hanging down her back in a braid. The kids would walk along behind her, mimicking her and pretending to look in the ash cans. Once Freddie found an old half-dead plant in an ash can. Vince dared him to give it to her. He rang the bell and she came out and said, Yes, what is it?

He said, Ma'am you want this?

We thought she'd slam the door but she took it as if he was giving her a present, and said, Thank you very much, it was very thoughtful of you. We nearly died laughing.

Then about a week later she knocked at our door. Mama came out and she had this plant in her hand and said, Mrs. Martin, one of the children gave me this plant and I was able to revive it. You have the morning sunshine and I wondered if you would like to give it a home.

So Mama took it and put it on the window sill, and what do you know? It started to have flowers! So Mama wanted to give it back to her and she wouldn't take it. She almost cried. She said, I don't think any woman should have to part with a plant in bloom.

Mama didn't want it, so she said, Well, I'll come and see it now and then. That satisfied Miss Clark and she took it. I don't think Mama ever went to visit the plant, though, on account of the smell.

See, Miss Clark had these two cats. She was crazy about them. She called them Alfred and Cassandra. She wouldn't let them out, and the smell in the house was terrible. People complained about it. Sometimes the cats would escape and she'd stand outside and call, Come back, Alfred! Come back, Cassandra! One time I grabbed one of them for her, and she was so grateful I thought she would cry. She asked me to come inside, and I nearly choked. I tried to think of something to say. I looked around at the plants all crowded together like a jungle, and I asked her, Miss Clark, why do you bring so many plants in here?

She reached up and touched one, sort of patted it, and said, They are alive. We must preserve life if we can.

I thought, Well, okay, but there's such a thing as too much.

One of the cats started climbing up a big plant, and she picked him off and said, No dear, you mustn't hurt the plants.

I started for the door, but then I saw the typewriter and I asked, Miss Clark, what do you write on the type-writer?

She said, In the daytime I do typing for people, and at night I write poems.

I said good-by and got out. I told Sharon about it and she said, I sure wish we could see those poems. I bet they're weird. Why don't you ask her?

I said I might, but I felt mean making fun of her, even if she was a little bit crazy. Still, it was always good for a laugh.

Well, it was getting pretty close to Christmas. One Saturday when I woke up, it was awfully cold. I was shivering in bed and wondering why my blankets didn't keep me warm, when Mama came in and closed the window and said, My goodness, it's like an icebox in the house. Papa is having trouble with the boiler.

And sure enough, the phone started ringing, people were complaining there was no heat. I got dressed, and pretty soon Sharon came running in shouting, It's snowing! Hey, Linda, it's snowing! Oh, excuse me, Mrs. Martin, I was so excited I forgot to say good morning.

Mama said, Good morning, I could do without the snow.

After a while Pop came in and said he thought he had fixed the boiler for the time being, but he would have to speak to the agent because we really needed a new boiler, this one wouldn't take much more patching. But now he was going out to shovel the sidewalk.

We went out too. The two lions looked as if they had white fur coats and hats on.

Sharon watched Pop shoveling. Then she said, Mr. Martin, can we help? Have you got another shovel?

Pop said, Sure but you don't want to shovel snow.

Yes, we do, she said. So Pop sent me down to the basement and I came back with two shovels. Sharon grabbed one and started pushing snow off the sidewalk.

Hey, this is fun, she said. I never get to shovel snow.

It was the first time I ever thought it was fun. We cleaned off the sidewalk and made a pile in the gutter. But suddenly Vince and Freddie and some other boys came along and started throwing snowballs at us. Sharon and I got behind our snow pile and threw back, and

48

pretty soon we were having a real snowball fight. Sharon could throw as hard as any boy. Carol came along and Sharon yelled at her, Come on, get in! Girls against the boys! So Carol joined us. She made the ammunition and Sharon and I fired the snowballs, and soon the whole sidewalk was covered with snow again.

Finally Vince hit a car—he didn't break anything but the man yelled at us to cut it out. So the boys said, Hey you girls are pretty good, want to go to the park?

Sharon said, Maybe, but first you clean this sidewalk off. We had it all clean and you messed it up.

So the boys got busy and cleaned it up. By then it was lunch time, and we went inside. Sharon came in to eat lunch. Pop was eating his lunch, talking to Mama about the boiler, but we didn't pay much attention. We were too hungry from all that snow fighting. We made sandwiches and took them in my room.

While we were eating, Sharon said, You know what, it's only a month till Christmas. I can hardly wait. I hope I get skis.

I thought, Skis! Oh, boy, that lets me out.

Sharon said, Maybe you could use my sister's old ones.

Well, then I started worrying about Christmas. Usually I only wondered what I was going to get, but suddenly I thought, I have to give her something, but how can I do it?

That night, I said, Mama, you know what, Christmas is coming.

Mama said, Is that news?

I said, Well, no, but I was thinking, I wish I could get something for Sharon.

Mama said, Sharon! That's all you think about. You better do your homework and get good marks. I don't like the way you're acting lately.

I thought to myself, She doesn't understand. And I shut up.

Mama said, Well, she'll probably give you something, so you better have something for her. How about some stockings?

I said, Oh, Mama, for heaven sake, she doesn't need stockings.

Mama said, She doesn't need anything, for that matter. It's just to show how you feel.

I thought, How I feel! Mama couldn't understand how I feel in a million years. I better shut up about the whole thing or I'll start to cry.

So I didn't say anything more. But I kept thinking, What can I get that she hasn't got, and that will be a big surprise?

I went to my room, and just as I was going to bed, Mama came in and said, Here. You can get something nice with this. And she gave me five dollars.

A few days later we were playing hide and seek in the building—Sharon and me and Carol and the boys, because after that snow fight we played with them. They said Sharon was as good as any boy. It was raining and cold and dark outside, so we played inside. Pop told us we could if we didn't bother anybody or break anything. Well, I ran down the basement stairs to hide, and suddenly I noticed the storeroom door was open. It was supposed to be kept locked because that was where the tenants stored their trunks and stuff. I thought it was a good place to hide so I went inside, and while I was waiting for them I looked around.

It was full of old trunks and boxes. They were all piled up with the apartment number over each pile. My Pop always arranged everything. That's how he is, everything where it belongs. One big pile had 1A on it. That must be the Plant Lady's stuff, I thought. I didn't know she had so much stuff. Probably she didn't have room for it in her apartment with all those plants. And right on top of a trunk was a guitar case. I could tell by the shape.

I thought, What is she doing with a guitar? Maybe there are some dried up old plants in it. I looked around to see if anybody was there, but it was all quiet. I opened the case, and inside was a guitar.

It was beautiful. It was even more beautiful than the one that Dave had. All shiny dark wood, with designs in lighter wood on the top. Just then I heard the kids coming. I shut the lid and hid behind a pile of trunks. Sharon was it, and she came rushing down yelling, Got you! But she really didn't know where I was. She looked all around but she never thought of looking in the storeroom. So finally I heard her say, Come on, I guess she's not here. Let's go back upstairs.

And I heard her and Vince go up the stairs. They were laughing about something. I had a funny feeling just then. I didn't like the idea of her and Vince laughing together like that. I liked it better when it was just Sharon and me. I thought, Okay, if she likes them so much I can get along.

I went and looked at the guitar again and it was just as beautiful as the first time. And suddenly, before I could even think what I was doing, I closed the case and picked it up and ran out of the storeroom with it. The

door slammed and locked behind me. Now what was I going to do? I looked around. There were some old refrigerators standing there, and I stuck the guitar inside one of them. Then I went upstairs.

The kids were all in the hall.

Where were you? they yelled at me. We couldn't find you. I said, I'm not telling. And I just looked mysterious. I could see they were dying to know where I was. But I said, I have to go now, and walked away.

Well, what was I going to do next? All the time I was eating supper and washing the dishes I was thinking, but I couldn't come up with an idea.

Well, after supper Pop takes a nap, so I told Mama I was going over to Sharon's to do homework, and I went down in the basement. I knew nobody would be there. I took the guitar out of the refrigerator and looked at it. It felt smooth and shiny, like silk. I plucked a string and it made a loud note. It sounded like a voice singing. Then I thought, Someone will hear. And I put my hand on it and the singing stopped.

I knew I should put it back where I got it, but the storeroom was locked. How could I ask Pop for the key? He'd want to know what for.

I put it away again and went upstairs. I thought, I'll go to Miss Clark and tell her I found it, and it had 1A on it in chalk, so I knew it was hers.

I had almost forgotten about wanting a guitar. Now all of a sudden it came back to me: if only I had one! I sat in my room thinking about it. I could almost feel that shiny smooth thing in my hands. I thought, Sharon can play tennis and ride horseback and climb mountains, but I can play the guitar. That's one thing she can't do. Her sister won't even let her touch hers.

I thought Sharon would really be impressed. I could offer to show her how to play. But then I had another idea. I didn't really want to impress her. I wanted to give her something. When you love somebody you want to give them the best thing there is. And what could I give her? She had everything—except a guitar. That's what I wanted to give her.

I decided I'd go to Miss Clark and see if she would let me work for her and earn it. That would be the thing. I would do it the next day. Right away I felt better, as if I had settled something.

But the next day I didn't have the nerve. How could I tell Miss Clark I found it? She would say, How come? Was it out of the storeroom? Wasn't the storeroom locked? She'd ask Pop about it and he'd get in trouble. I was nearly going crazy.

All day in school I was worrying about it. On the way home Sharon kept talking to me and I hardly answered. Finally she said, Linda, what's the matter with you?

I said, Oh, I'm thinking about Christmas.

She said, Me too, and I tell you what, I'm going downtown shopping on Saturday. You want to come?

I said, I don't know if I can. (I was thinking I might get a chance to talk to Miss Clark.) Carol was walking with us and she said, Oh, I'd like to go. I love shopping downtown.

So they made a date to go. Then I started to feel jealous and wished I could go. But I couldn't say anything then.

We got to the house, and just as I was going in the apartment a man came in from outside and said, Where's the Super?

I said, Who wants him? He said, We got an order to take away some junk.

I saw a big truck outside. I went in and Pop was drinking coffee. He saw the man and called out, They're down in the basement. Go through the alley, I'll be right with you.

The man went away and I asked Pop, Who is he?

He said, I'm getting rid of some old iceboxes, got to clear out the junk.

Well, I almost died. Honestly, my heart almost stopped beating. I rushed out the door and down the cellar stairs. The men were going around by the alley, so I got there first.

I pulled open the refrigerator door and grabbed the guitar and rushed back upstairs to my room. It was just luck that I didn't meet anybody. I shoved the guitar in my closet and threw some clothes on top. Then I sat down on the bed to catch my breath. I was breathing so hard and my heart was beating so fast I thought I'd faint, but I didn't. After a while I went in the kitchen and got a glass of milk.

That night, I could hardly go to sleep. There I was in the bed, and right in the same room, about five feet away, was the guitar. I couldn't stop thinking about it. I tried to imagine that it was mine, and that I could take it out and play it. I sat up in bed. The moon was shining in the window. I shivered. It was awfully cold. Suddenly I had a terrible thought. That guitar in the closet wasn't mine. It belonged to Miss Clark and I had taken it. Well, let's face it: stolen it. I shivered again but not from cold. Finally I fell asleep.

THE next day was Friday, the last day before Christmas vacation. We didn't have any homework, and everybody was happy—everybody except me, I guess. The kids were all talking about what they were going to get for Christmas, and the teachers let us talk, they didn't bother with school work. We played games, and our home room teacher had a box of candy for us. We got out after lunch.

As we were walking home, Sharon said, You know what? I'm going to have a party. All the kids must come. It'll be the day before Christmas Eve, and we'll trim the tree. Won't that be great?

I said, Uh-huh. But I thought to myself, I haven't got enough to worry about, now I have to think what I'll wear.

Sharon said, It looks like more snow. I hope we get a lot. Then we can go skiing in the park. Hey, let's go this afternoon if it snows, and you can use my old skis and I'll borrow Betsy's.

But I said, No, I have to go home. I have to help my mother.

Sharon said, Okay, I'll go with you. I'll help you with your work, then you'll get through sooner.

I said, No, I have to go somewhere.

She looked at me and said, What's the matter with you? You mad at me or something?

I shook my head no. I couldn't tell her I was wondering how to talk to Miss Clark. But when we got to the Almont, there was Miss Clark out on the stoop, shivering in her sweater. She was calling, Here, kitty! Here, Alfred!

There was Alfred down in the alley, and a big mean old street cat was growling at him.

I said, Wait, I'll catch him.

I ran into the house and grabbed the first thing I could find, which was a laundry basket. I ran out the back way and into the alley. Alfred was still there, with his tail and all his fur swelled out like a balloon. The mean old cat was just going to jump on him, when I plopped the basket down on top of Alfred. He let out a screech, but I stuck my hand in and grabbed him by the fur. He scratched me, but I held on to him and reached him up to Miss Clark through the fence. She hugged him and talked to him and there were tears in her eyes.

Then I realized all the kids were standing around laughing and watching me. Sharon yelled, Linda, the wild animal tamer!

I ran back through the alley and into the apartment. I didn't want to talk to them.

But later, when I was going out, Miss Clark put her head out and said, Linda, come in just a moment, please.

I went in, and the smell was so bad I could hardly stand it. I thought no wonder the cats want to get out. But Miss Clark didn't seem to notice. She had three plants on a table, and she said Alfred and I are so grateful, we want you to choose a plant. Which one would you like?

Well, all I wanted was to get out, on account of the smell and the cats rubbing against my legs. I grabbed the first one and said, This one is nice, thanks.

Then I remembered that this was my chance to talk to her, only I hadn't planned what I would say. I said the first thing that came into my head. I said, Miss Clark, I wanted to ask you something. Once I was down in the storeroom and I saw a guitar case. Was that yours?

She said, That was my sister's. She was a wonderful person. I keep it in memory of her. It is very precious to me.

So that was my answer. I took the plant and got out. I brought it into the house and gave it to Mama.

She said, What's this? And I explained that Miss Clark gave it to me, because I caught her cat. Mama said, Well, that's nice but don't get too friendly. Just be polite, that's all. My goodness, it's cold. Brr!

She was looking worried, but I didn't pay any attention. I was thinking that I better go shopping with my five dollars and figure out what to do with the guitar later.

Just then somebody knocked at the door. Mama opened it, and it was Mrs. Ferguson. She had her lips pressed together and her chin sticking out as if she was real angry. She said, Mrs. Martin, it is very cold in this house. There is no heat in my radiator.

Mama said, Well, what can we do? Light the oven.

Mrs. Ferguson said, I do not approve of lighting the oven. It is dangerous.

Then she pressed her lips together and went away. But soon she came back, and said, And another thing. The tenant in the front apartment is not clean. Every time her door opens, an odor can be detected.

I wanted to laugh, not about the smell, but the way she described it, as if she was the queen or somebody. And I wanted to laugh at myself too, making up fairy tales about giving Sharon a guitar. What a dope.

The next morning I went shopping. I decided I'd go to one of the big stores downtown. I walked down Fifth Avenue looking at the windows decorated with a million lights and Christmas ornaments shining and whirling around till I almost got dizzy. And the things in the windows! Toys and clothes and jewelry and I don't know what.

I thought, I can't go inside one of those places. They'll say, What are you doing here?

Then I got up my nerve and went in. I walked around looking at things. I felt as if the salesladies were watching me. They said, Yes, dear, what would you like? I thought, Well, I'd like this and this and this. Then I looked at some of the prices and almost ran out.

But suddenly I got an idea. I'd get Sharon something for skiing. I went to the ski department and looked at the stuff there. Boots that cost fifty dollars! Skis that cost a hundred! Well, finally I found a pair of mittens. They were wool, all different colors. I thought she could use them.

The lady wrapped them in gold paper with a red ribbon. It looked pretty neat.

Then I thought, What'll I give Mama? I had about two dollars of my own, and I had nothing for Joe and Pop. I walked around and finally I saw a box of cookies for two dollars. I thought they could all have some, and I got that. Then I went home.

When I came out of the subway it was snowing. Big flakes, that looked as if a lot of feathers were falling out of the sky. I thought, Sharon will be glad. She can go skiing. I went home and put away my packages. I stuck them in the closet with the guitar and piled some more stuff on top.

Well, it snowed all night and the next day. It was a blizzard. Everything was covered with snow. It looked beautiful. That is, you would think so if your father was not a Super. For him it just meant trouble. He had to shovel the sidewalk and the steps so nobody should fall down, and keep the furnace going, and put the garbage out. Joe had a day off from the garage and he stayed home and helped Pop.

I wasn't much help. I hadn't heard from Sharon for about three days and I wondered if she was mad at me. I was sort of moping around the house waiting for her to call me about the party. But she didn't.

So finally I called her. Some strange woman's voice answered the phone and when I asked for Sharon she called out, Miss Sharon! It's for you. Sharon came to the phone and her voice sounded strange too. I couldn't figure out what was the matter. I said, Do you want to come over? She said, No, I can't.

I said, Well, should I come over there?

She said, Wait a minute. I could hear her talking to somebody. Then she said, Yes, come over.

So I went. I took my present along. Sharon let me in and when I looked at her I knew why her voice sounded queer. She had been crying! I was so surprised I almost flipped. I never imagined Sharon crying. I don't know why not, everybody cries sometimes, but she was always so cheerful. We went in her room, and the strange woman came and said how do you do to me. Sharon said she was a housekeeper.

I said, I didn't know you had a housekeeper. She said, Well, my mother has gone away.

I said, Where? What for?

Then she said that her father and mother were going to get a divorce, and this woman was keeping house

64

for her father and sister, and she was going to go away to school.

I don't know when I ever felt so terrible. It felt as if everything in my life was falling apart. Of course it wasn't my life, it was Sharon's. But I had sort of imagined that it was mine. I wanted to shout out, They can't! It's not right! Only of course it was none of my business.

In one way it was, though, because Sharon was my friend, and she was sitting there with her eyes red and her head hanging down, just limp. It wasn't like her at all.

I said, But what's it all about? I thought your family was the greatest.

She said, So did I. Well, I guess they still are, but not as a family. Mother's going to marry somebody else.

And she gave a sigh. I wish I didn't have to go to another school, she said. I sure liked it at this school, with you and all the other kids, and going to the park, and your house. Gee, that was the best part.

I thought, Imagine that! She lives in a place like this and she thinks my house is the best part.

She said, Well, the thing is, the party is off. I'm sorry.

I said, Well, we'll still have Christmas, won't we?

She said, No. I have to go to my grandmother's for Christmas. I'm going tomorrow.

Well, I almost started to cry at that. I couldn't stand it. But Sharon said, So I want to give you your present now. And she handed me a long flat package, and a square package. The square one is for your mother, she said. Well, really for your whole family.

Then I gave her her present and she said, Let's open them, I can't wait. She tore hers open and when she saw the mittens she said, They're great! Just what I need for school. It's in Vermont and it's cold there.

Then I opened mine and it was a tennis racket. It was so beautiful that I cried, and then Sharon cried, and we hugged each other and just howled.

Sharon stopped first and said, I'll walk you home. So we went out. We heard bells clanging and sirens.

I said, There's a fire someplace. We followed the sound and there were the engines right in my street. We started to run. It was the Almont! The engines were out in front, and the firemen were going in with hoses and axes. Smoke was coming out of an upstairs window. People were looking out of the windows. Pop was on the sidewalk and people were pulling his arm and saying, What happened, Super? The cops were pushing everybody back.

Sharon said, Boy, this is exciting. I'm glad I came out.

Pretty soon the firemen came out and rolled up their hoses and went away. It was great the way they did everything. There was a black and white dog on one of the engines. He sat there as if he was watching to see they didn't forget anything.

Pop said that somebody had lit the oven to keep warm, and some towels had caught fire.

Sharon and I went inside and she said good-by to Mama. She gave Mama the square package and said Merry Christmas and Happy New Year. Then she gave Mama a kiss and ran out. I went too, and walked back to her house. We stood around for a few minutes and Sharon said, I'll write to you.

Then we kissed each other good-by—it was the first time I ever kissed her, and the last time too—and I ran home feeling as if the bottom had dropped out of everything.

8

CHRISTMAS Day, I didn't want to wake up. But it was so cold in my room, I had to come out. The kitchen was warm from the oven. We opened our presents there.

Joe had bought things for me and Mama and Pop. He bought me a red sweater that was really great. Mama had made me a skirt to go with it, and a bathrobe. Pop gave me five dollars. I felt as if I didn't deserve any of it.

Mama liked my cookies and when she opened Sharon's package it was a fruit cake. She said it was nice to have those things in the house in case company came, and Pop said, Why do we need company? We can eat them ourselves.

Then he went down to the cellar and shook up the furnace, and it got a little warmer, and people came to the door with Christmas money and cards. Mr. Berger brought a bottle of whiskey. Pop had some and gave some to Joe. He was going to give me some but Mama said, Sam! I didn't like the smell anyhow.

Mama baked chicken and a pie, and we all had dinner together in the dining room, and sat in front of the TV and watched a Christmas program. I started to feel a little better.

Then I thought I'd go out so I put on my new things and walked down the street toward Sharon's house. I thought maybe she would still be there and I'd see her once more, but I didn't. I felt as if I was all alone and there wasn't anything in the world worth doing. I might as well go home again.

On the way I saw something under a car. Something moving just a little. It was a baby pigeon—a creepy-looking thing, with hardly any feathers, and a big ugly mouth. I don't know how it got there, but I had to do something with it. I couldn't let it stay there in the dirty snow. I picked it up and put it in my scarf and then I thought, Now what? I can't take this in the house.

Suddenly I remembered Miss Clark. She was nutty enough to take pity on it. I took it in and knocked at her door and said, Look what I found.

She took it in her hands and smoothed it, just as if it was some lovely creature, not a disgusting naked half-dead thing. She talked to it and said, It's cold and hungry. We'll warm it up. She warmed the oven and

70

then turned off the heat and put it in there with the door open, till it opened its eyes. Then she fed it some bread soaked in milk. I saw when she opened the icebox to take out a can of milk, that there was almost nothing there. She said she'd keep the pigeon.

I went home and asked Mama if there was anything left over from dinner that I could give her for her cats, and Mama gave me a bag of scraps. I wouldn't be surprised if Miss Clark ate them herself.

And every time I thought about her, I'd be reminded of that guitar in my closet, that I ought to do something about. But it was as if I was paralyzed. I couldn't do anything.

We had a week of Christmas vacation left, but I had nothing to do, so I stayed in the house. I helped Mama. I did the ironing, and Mama had a piece of material that some tenant had given her and we made a dress for school.

Pop wasn't in much. Mostly he was down in the basement. He'd come up for lunch and go down again. It was quiet in the house, just the sewing machine going in the dining room, and me ironing in the living room with the TV on, and now and then the doorbell or the phone would ring and Mama would stop sewing and answer it. I wasn't paying much attention but all of a sudden I thought, Gee, they're ringing that bell an awful lot, what's going on?

Then I started to listen. I heard somebody say, It's very cold here, Mrs. Martin, can't you do something about it? And Mama would say, What can I do? My husband is doing all he can. And the person would say, Well, we can't take this, we'll all be getting pneumonia. And Mama would say, Well, all I can do is tell my husband.

I asked Mama what was going on and she said, Where have you been, on the moon or someplace? Didn't you notice there isn't any heat?

And to tell the truth I hadn't. First I was out so much, and then I was feeling so bad, I just didn't think about anybody else. I said, No, I noticed it was cold but I thought it was the weather.

She said, Yes, the weather and something else. The boiler has a big crack in it and the furnace is no good, and Pop can't fix it. They need a new boiler and new parts and when he tells the agent about it he says they won't spend the money. Those lousy—

She was getting madder and madder, her voice was shaking, and finally she said a word I never heard my mother say before. Then the doorbell rang again and she said a swear word and opened the door and said, Yes, what is it now?

It was somebody else complaining. The hot water was cold, and there was no heat, almost a month now there had been practically no heat.

Then Pop came in for lunch. His face was dirty from the furnace and he didn't even wash, he just sat down at the table all slumped over and gave a sigh. I looked at him and thought, My goodness, he was so happy about this job and now look at him!

72

I said, What's the matter, Pop?

He said, What's the matter? I can't fix a house with nothing, that's all.

And he started to eat. But then he stopped eating and just sat there.

Well, it got worse, because the weather got colder. We were really having a cold wave. And the tenants complained more and more. They complained about other things while they were at it. They said the stoves were out of order and the windows rattled and the pipes leaked and the sinks were stopped up. One night the snow melted on the roof and the water ran into the electric wires and started another fire. The firemen came and put it out but we had no lights.

And they didn't only complain about the house. Even more they complained about each other. Mrs. Keating complained that Mr. Berger caught her son Freddie fooling around in the basement, and said it was none of his business, and the Bergers said Mrs. Quinn's roomers left garbage in the hall. And Mrs. Ferguson complained about the Lopezes. She said they made too much noise over her head. They really did make a lot of noise. New Year's Eve they had a party and were dancing and carrying on all night, and Mrs. Ferguson said her ceiling cracked on account of it.

Maybe she was right, it was some party. I know because Carol invited me to come. Her mother invited all of us, but Mama didn't want to go. She was too upset, and didn't feel like celebrating.

But I had a good time, and Carol and I got to be friends, I mean more than we were before. Her brother Vince was there, and Freddie Keating, and some more kids. We all danced and had a lot to eat, and at midnight when the horns started blowing they began kissing each other and drinking everybody's health.

Vince got excited, he must have had some beer or wine, and he grabbed me and kissed me, and Freddie kissed Carol. In the middle of all this, there was this banging on the pipes. That meant Mrs. Ferguson didn't like the noise.

Carol's mother said, Oh, that Mrs. Ferguson, she's the limit. Can you imagine that on New Year's Eve? Don't pay any attention.

But Mrs. Ferguson must have called the Super, because Pop came in yawning, I guess he had been asleep.

They all shouted, Oh, here's the Super, come on in, Super, and have a drink, and Pop laughed and said it was a good party, even if it was cold they worked up enough heat so they didn't feel it. I thought how Sharon would have laughed.

But the next day it was colder than ever. Some pipes froze, and Pop was down in the cellar with a kettle of hot water trying to thaw them out. But he didn't get there soon enough because they cracked. Then we had a leak, and try to get a plumber on New Year's Day!

People would meet each other in the hall all bundled up and say, Isn't this terrible! Well, what can we do about it?

Then Mr. Berger decided there was something he could do. He wrote a letter to the Housing Department. It said there had been no heat for weeks, and some people had no water on account of the pipes freezing, and there had been fires on account of the bad wiring, and all things like that. He went around to all the tenants to get them to sign it.

Some didn't want to, they were afraid. He said to them, There is nothing to be afraid of, it is the law.

Then some said they didn't want to hurt the Super, because he was a good Super and did his best, and he said, It is nothing against the Super, it is the owners, who won't spend the money to fix things. So finally most people signed, and he sent it away.

After that a man came to see Pop. He said he was from the City, and some of the tenants had sent in a complaint. People were in the hall trying to find out what was happening. When they heard the man was from the City, they all started complaining about the building and he wrote it all down. He went to every apartment and looked to see what was the matter. Only when he came to Miss Clark she wouldn't let him in. Then Mrs. Ferguson, who was there with her hat and gloves on, said that apartment was the worst of the lot and was a health hazard.

Then she rang our bell and said to Mama, One of the tenants has entered a complaint against the building. The building is all right, it is just the people who live in it, my husband would never have stood for it, they are all troublemakers and probably Communists and I shall write to the authorities. I shall complain about the people who riot all night.

Mama said, Yes, ma'am, and closed the door. I said, What is going to happen now? Mama said, Nothing is going to happen. We are just going to mind our own business. That man who was here wrote everything down but he isn't going to do anything. They never do. So go and play and tell the kids not to make too much noise because Pop isn't feeling too well.

I didn't feel like going out, I just wanted to go in my room and write a letter to Sharon. I had it all planned out in my mind, all the funny things I would tell her about the party, and what a pest Mrs. Ferguson was, and the rest.

But suddenly there was a noise in the hall, people yelling and running, and Mama and I ran out, and Mrs. Ferguson had fallen on the stairs. Pop came and picked her up, but she had fainted or something, anyhow she was unconscious.

Mama said, Don't touch her, just call an ambulance. But Mrs. Lopez came running down and said, Mr. Martin, just take her upstairs to her apartment and I'll take care of her. I know what to do, it happened before.

Pop carried her up and somebody got her door open and they laid her down on the bed. I looked around her apartment. It had almost nothing in it. It had a few pictures on the wall, sort of Japanese or Chinese, I'm not sure which, and a couple of chairs and a table. The chairs and table were beautiful, old, and polished, like Sharon's furniture. And in the bedroom was just the bed and a chest of drawers with little pieces of mother-of-pearl set into the wood. But that was all, no rugs, no couch, no nothing.

Just the opposite of Miss Clark, where there was such a mess you could hardly walk in. And it was as cold as ice. She didn't even have the oven lit, the way most of us did.

Mrs. Lopez said everybody should get out, and she would take over. So Carol and I went up to her apartment and we talked. It felt good to have somebody to talk to again. I could stop thinking about Sharon for a while. You know how it feels when you have been seeing somebody nearly every day and telling them every single thing, and then suddenly they disappear? It feels as if part of you was missing. You look for it and it isn't there. That's how I felt.

Carol understood that, she said, Gee, you must miss Sharon, she was a lot of fun. I used to envy her because she had such a lot of things, but I guess I don't need to envy her any more, after all I have my family, and so do you.

Well, after a while Mrs. Lopez came up and got some soup and bread and milk. She was going back to Mrs. Ferguson's apartment with them. She took some blankets too.

Carol said, What are those for, Ma?

She said, She has no heat, her gas is turned off. She didn't pay the bill.

Carol said, But is something the matter with her?

And her mother said, She was practically starving, that's all.

Well, can you imagine that?

# 9

Sᴄʜᴏᴏʟ started again. Carol and I and sometimes the boys went together. The weather was terrible. Cold and cloudy and sometimes snow and freezing rain. Pop was always putting sand on the sidewalk so nobody should fall and break a leg. We didn't play outside. It was too nasty. We found a little room under the stairs that was supposed to be for baby carriages or something. Nobody used it so we played there. We squeezed in and played cards.

And I wrote letters to Sharon. When I got home from school the first thing I would do was to look for the mail, but there wasn't any. Then one day I got a postcard. It had a picture of a white house on it with trees all around and a tennis court. On the back Sharon had written: Dear Linda, this is my school. It's great.

Lots of skiing and not too much math. Will write more soon. Love, Sharon.

That was all.

I went into my room and looked at the tennis racket. I wondered what it would be like to go to a school like that. I remembered a movie I saw once on TV, about a girls' school. The girls all wore the same uniform, gray with white blouses, and for tennis they wore short white dresses. They got packages from home with cake and fruit, and at night they would have parties in their rooms and sing and play guitars.

At that I had a shock. I had almost forgotten the guitar. I felt in the back of the closet. It was there but I didn't take it out. I closed the door and tried to forget it again.

I thought, Oh, well, pretty soon spring will come and it will get warm and everybody will feel better.

Then I heard Pop come in. He walked into the kitchen and sat down and I heard Mama say, Sam! What's the matter?

Pop mumbled something and Mama said, No!

I came out of my room and there was Pop at the table and Mama standing there staring at him.

I said, What happened?

Pop just hunched up his shoulders.

I thought maybe he was sick. I said, Pop! What's the matter?

Mama said, The house is sold.

I said, What? What do you mean?

Mama said, Pop just got the news. They sold the house, and we'll have to move.

I looked from one to the other and said, But why?

Mama said, Linda, will you please stop asking stupid questions? Go and play or do something.

I said, But I mean why do we have to move if the house is sold? Why can't we stay here even if somebody else owns it?

Mama said, Because the new owner is going to make everybody move, then he's going to rebuild the whole house, make it all modern. It'll be a luxury apartment.

I said, Hm! I thought all we needed was a new boiler.

Pop said, They'll get a new boiler but we won't be here.

I asked him, When do we have to move?

And he said, In sixty days. Then he sighed, and leaned his head on his hand. I couldn't look at him. I went out in the hall. I thought, Just when we get a decent place to live, we have to get out. Now we'll go back to one of those broken-down dumps with rats and garbage in the hall. Why do we have to take this?

I started to get mad. I forgot that a little while ago I was calling the Almont a dump and envying Sharon her fancy private school. And ever since I met Sharon I had been looking at the way she lived and wishing my father didn't have to mop floors and put out trash.

I leaned against the bannister that Pop had fixed and thought, I guess they'll take it away and burn it up. It's not fair. There ought to be something we can do. Why can't Pop do something? He's a grownup.

But Pop couldn't do anything. He could only take it and go.

Then the kids came down, Carol and Vince and the others. They were all excited and scared because their folks had told them the news.

Carol said, Hi, Linda, did you hear?

I said, Yes, I heard. I don't want to move. What can we do?

Vince said, What can anybody do? It's their building.

Just then we heard an argument going on. We went up to see what it was all about. Mrs. Ferguson was out in the hall. She looked a little better because Mrs. Lopez had been bringing her meals, but she was still pretty skinny and sour-looking. She and the red-headed woman and Mrs. Quinn were arguing. Mrs. Ferguson said that if the tenants had behaved themselves and had not complained to the Housing and the Agent, this would not have happened.

Fifty-one years I've lived here, she said. Now I've got to move on account of people like you!

The red-headed woman said, People like us! Well, how do you like that! I suppose you think you're better than us!

Just then Mrs. Lopez came down and said, Oh, have you heard the news? What'll I do with all my kids?

Then Mrs. Ferguson said, If your children didn't make so much noise we might get a better class of tenant in here, not all that riff-raff.

And Mrs. Quinn said, That's a fine way to talk after

that lady was so good to you! That's gratitude from her majesty. And as to riff-raff, I could tell a few things about you, ma'am!

I wondered what she meant but then some people began coming home from work, some of Mrs. Quinn's roomers, and the crippled girl's mother, and they were all shouting, and then somebody said, It's all that fellow Berger's fault. He's the one that sent the complaint to the Housing. He's the one that ought to get out.

And somebody else said, Yes, that's right, if we let the owner alone and didn't complain so much he wouldn't have to spend so much fixing up the house and he wouldn't want to sell it.

Carol started to giggle, but I just got madder. I said to her, They make me sick acting like that. They were all complaining before but he's the only one that did anything.

Carol looked at me and said, What's with you?

I said, Somebody around here must have some sense. Come on, I'm going to do something.

I don't know what got into me, but I marched down the stairs and knocked at Mr. Berger's door. The kids followed me and stood there behind me.

He opened the door and said, Yes, what can I do for you?

I said, Mr. Berger, Can you figure out something to do?

He stood there for a minute as if he was making up his mind what to say. Then he said, Do about what?

I said, About us getting kicked out of this building.

He said, You want me to do something?

I said, Yes, didn't you hear? The house is sold, and we will all have to move out. You were the one that sent a letter to the Housing so you must know what to do.

He said, Why should I?

I said, Why? So all these people shouldn't have to move.

He said, Why shouldn't they move? They don't care about me. They don't do anything for themselves. They just gripe. Why should you ask me to do anything?

I thought, He's right. Why should he? Nobody cares about him. Even me, all I care about is my own family.

I said, My father will be out of a job. We'll have to go back to one of those awful places full of roaches and rats and garbage. We'll have to live in two rooms and not be able to go out in the street. I don't want to. I won't. I want to stay here.

By this time I was almost yelling. Suddenly I looked at Carol and Vince and Freddie, and they were staring at me as if I was crazy. Carol said, Linda, take it easy, and she put her hand on my arm.

But I shook it off and said, I won't take it easy. I won't. They all make me sick. Mr. Berger's right. They just gripe and fight each other and don't do anything. I hate them!

And I started to cry.

Mr. Berger stood there staring at me, and the kids too, and finally I managed to stop and said, Excuse me, Mr. Berger. I shouldn't have bothered you. Forget it. And I ran downstairs. I called, So long, to the kids and went into the apartment, leaving them out there looking worried.

Joe was home and Mama was giving him supper and telling him what happened. I went in the bathroom to wash my face before Mama could see it and ask me what I was crying about. Suddenly there was a knock on the door. Mama called to me to go because she was busy. And there was Mr. Berger.

He said, Is your father here?

I thought, Oh boy, now he's coming to tell Pop that I went to him, and Pop will be in trouble and then I'll get it.

I said, I'll call my mother.

So Mama came and he said, Mrs. Martin, I have been thinking about this eviction notice. It is all wrong to give people sixty days notice and we should protest.

Mama said, What do you want to do?

So he said, I would like to call a meeting of all the tenants. We could have it in my apartment. Then we could decide what to do.

Mama looked scared. She said, Well, I'll ask my husband. I'll let you know tomorrow what he says.

But Mr. Berger said, Excuse me, but I would like to see him right now.

Joe got up from the table and came to the door and said, I think you're right, Mr. Berger, I'll get my father.

Pretty soon Pop came up from the basement with Joe. Joe was talking to him, and Pop was walking slowly, dragging his feet as if he was very tired.

Mr. Berger explained to him all over again. He didn't say a word about me, and was I glad!

Then Mama said, But we don't want to get into trouble.

Joe looked impatient and said, What trouble?

Mama said, He might get fired.

Joe said, But he's fired already, Mama, use your head, why don't you?

Mama said, Yes, but if he makes trouble he won't get a reference, and how could he get another job?

All of a sudden something seemed to happen to Pop. He looked at Joe, and at Mr. Berger, and he said, Fired? Of course I'm fired. So what? What have we got to lose? Come on in, Mr. Berger.

So they sat down at the table to decide what to do. They wrote on pieces of paper: Come to a meeting in my apartment tomorrow night to discuss steps to be taken to protest eviction.

Then Mr. Berger said, No, better make it tonight. Better not waste time.

Then Carol and I and the boys went around delivering the papers. Some of the tenants looked suspicious when they saw Mr. Berger's name. But that night they all came, even the crippled girl. Her father brought her in the wheel chair. It was his night off, and he explained his wife was tired.

Mr. Berger's living room was pretty crowded. People had to bring in extra chairs.

Then Mr. Berger stood up in front and said, Neighbors, you all got notices to move. If we all act together maybe we can do something.

Mrs. Lopez said, What can we do? It's his building.

But Mr. Berger said, The law says that you can't throw people out until they find another place.

Then somebody said, That's right! I heard of that. It's the urban renewal. First they have to find a place.

One of the roomers said, But the owner got permission from the Housing, didn't he?

Okay, Mr. Berger said. That's why we need a lawyer, to show that it's wrong. I have a friend who is a lawyer. If you like I'll speak to him and we'll go to court.

Then everybody started talking at once. Lawyers cost money. Nobody has money to spare. And anyhow, how do we know who this lawyer is? What's Mr. Berger doing this for? (I was close enough to hear somebody whisper that.)

Then Mrs. Lopez stood up—she was pretty fat so when she stood up you could see her. And she said, Look, we might as well chip in and get a lawyer. If we don't, we'll just have to move and then what? Where will we get a place like this? It's true the roof leaks and there's no heat, but it's not a bad place. There's plenty of room and nice people.

So finally they decided that everybody would chip in a few dollars, and Mr. Berger got his friend the lawyer, and we all signed a petition. (Not the kids, of course, though we cared just as much as the grownups.) A few people were afraid to sign, but Pop told them not to be afraid. The petition asked the court to let us stay in the house. We sent it away, and then we began to wait for an answer. It took a long time to come. But finally it came, and it said we should come to court for a hearing.

Then they all got excited again, deciding who should go. Mr. Berger said everybody should go, even if they had to miss a day of work. So we all went, and Joe stayed home from his job to mind the building. He really wanted to go and see the fun but he stayed. We all wore our best clothes, and we got a few taxis and all went together.

It was almost like a picnic. Of course everybody was worried, but still they were enjoying themselves. They were kidding and saying things like, Hey, Mrs. Lopez, you're too fat, you take enough room for three people. And Mrs. Lopez said, Okay, two can sit on my lap.

When we got there, we all sat in a row in the court-room, and the Judge came in. He had on a black robe, just like on television. He banged on the desk with a hammer, and a man at a table said, Hear ye, hear ye. Draw nigh and you shall be heard. It sounded just like a movie.

Then the Judge asked us to tell why we thought we should not have to move. So the lawyer explained how many children and old people lived in the house, and

about the crippled girl and the woman who took roomers, and about the poor people who couldn't afford to pay more rent.

But the owner was there too, the one who bought the house. He said he was going to tear down the whole house, not just fix it up. He said the house was in bad condition and couldn't be fixed up.

The Judge said, You mean it is not fit for human habitation?

Then Pop got up. He said the house would be perfectly all right if it had some repairs. So the Judge said he would send people to inspect it. Meantime the owner was not to do anything.

Then we all went home, feeling pretty good. We were all talking and laughing, and the red-headed lady said, Well, we sure told them, didn't we?

Then Mrs. Lopez said, You know, I have a pot of chili home. If anybody wants to share it, they're welcome.

Well, somebody else had some cans of fruit and beer and cake and we all got together and had a party. Even Mrs. Ferguson came, but Miss Clark wouldn't. I forgot to say she didn't come to court either. Somebody said she had no decent clothes to wear. You can't go to court in a sweater and sneakers.

At the party, Mr. Berger was sitting by himself in a corner, and I said, Mr. Berger, you're the one who did everything.

Then the others heard me and said, Yes, we better thank Mr. Berger.

But he said, Wait, don't be in such a hurry, we don't know anything yet. They are going to send inspectors to look at the building.

Then Mrs. Lopez said, We ought to clean it up so they will see it's a nice place. We can't leave it all to the Super.

So the next day we all got together and worked. We cleaned and threw out a lot of garbage, and it looked great. If somebody saw a kid throw a can or a paper on the floor, they would say, Hey, pick that up, no littering!

Mrs. Ferguson said it looked just the way it used to look when her husband was alive. Honestly, one time she almost smiled. Oh, by the way, I asked Carol what Mrs. Quinn meant that time when they were fighting, and she said her mother heard that Mr. Ferguson wasn't such a saint, he got kicked out of his missionary job for something he did, but she didn't know what.

Well, then we waited for the inspectors. And the whole time we waited, the people kept telling each other, It's got to be Yes.

At last the inspectors came. They came in the morning while we were at school, so we didn't see them.
But Mama said they went over the place with a fine
tooth comb. They looked at all the violations and Pop
told them how they could be fixed. Then they went
away and we had to wait for the answer. It seemed like
we waited forever. It was getting to be spring. The
snow melted and it was nice out.

One day Carol and I walked down to the river where
I used to go with Sharon. I told Carol how Sharon said
she wanted to climb mountains and be a captain of a
ship, and Carol said, Well, she was a nice kid and had
some good ideas, but in a way I'm glad she left.

I asked why and she said, Because this way you and
I can be friends.

I was quite surprised at that, I didn't know she liked me that much, but I said, Yes, I'm glad we are, and I hope if we have to move we'll still see each other sometimes.

Then we went home, and wouldn't you know, that day the answer came from the court and it was—No.

We had to go. The Judge said that the man who bought the property had a right to do what he wanted. But—we had time. He couldn't start demolishing till everybody was out. We had time to look.

So one by one the families moved. Every couple of months, somebody would say, Well, folks, we found something in Brooklyn, or, We found something in the Bronx. And we would all go out and say good-by, wave and call good luck, and off they would go.

One day, Mama decided she better start getting ready to move. It's true we didn't have a place yet, but Pop was looking, and he might find one any day.

That day I came home from school, and Mama called to me, Linda, come here. She was in my room.

And before I even got there I knew what she wanted.

She said to me, What is this? Where did you get this guitar?

My heart pounded so hard I thought I would faint. I never had figured out what to do with it or what to say, but it came to me all of a sudden. I said, The lady in 1A lent it to me.

She *lent* it to you! What for?

I said, I was telling her that I wished I could play

94

a guitar, and she said, I have one that I don't use, you can borrow it.

Mama said, Well, I never heard you play it. What's it doing in the closet?

I said, I didn't want the kids to know, they'd tell everybody.

Mama said, Well, you better take it back now. I think I'll go with you.

I said, You don't need to.

But she said, Come on.

She rang the bell and Miss Clark came out looking all messy with her hair hanging down.

Mama pushed me inside and said, Go ahead.

I almost died. I said, Miss Clark, I told Mama you lent me this guitar and now I'm giving it back.

My throat hurt so I could hardly talk.

I held it out to her and said, Thank you.

I waited for her to say, Well, I never lent it to you. I thought it was down in the storeroom. But she didn't. She just stood there as if she was trying to remember something.

Then she said, Why, Linda, you misunderstood me. I didn't lend it to you. I gave it to you. It's yours.

The way she said it, nobody would think about how she looked, or that her house was a mess. She was so dignified and calm, she seemed to get taller, somehow.

I almost couldn't breathe. I held out the guitar and said, No, it isn't mine.

She said, Yes, it is. I want you to have it. It will be a

remembrance from me and Alfred and Cassandra. Good-by, dear.

And she leaned forward and kissed me on the cheek. Then she patted the guitar case as if she was saying good-by to it too. And Mama and I went out and she shut the door. Mama gave me a funny look but didn't say anything.

I was like in a dream. I couldn't believe it. I felt so ashamed. But at the same time I felt relieved. It wasn't just that I could keep the guitar. It was that she was telling me she liked me.

Then I said to Mama, What did she mean by good-by? Is she moving? Did she find a place?

Mama said, She has to go to a home. She can't live alone any more, and besides she can't pay the rent. She hasn't paid in months.

I said, What kind of a home? Mama said, You know, a home for old people, where she'll be taken care of.

I thought, I bet they won't let her go out and collect a lot of half-dead plants. I asked, What will she do with the plants and cats?

Mama said, Get rid of them, most likely.

The next day I thought maybe I'd ask for one of her plants to keep. But when I went out in the hall, there she was coming out of her door. She didn't see me. She had a basket with a lid on it. It was heavy and something inside said, Meow!

She said, Be quiet. She went out and got in a taxi. I didn't see her come back in a taxi. Probably she walked.

And soon after that she went away for good.

Pop had to call the junk men to take away all the stuff. He said the apartment was the worst mess he ever saw. I asked him if I could have a plant, and he said, All right, but don't get like Miss Clark. So I went in and took a small one, and while I was looking I saw a little cardboard box on the floor. I opened it and in it was a dead baby pigeon. It was all dried up, and didn't even smell.

And on the floor I saw some sheets of paper with typing on them. I picked them up and they were covered with poetry. So I took them home and put them in a box. I couldn't bear to read them right then. But later I did. Some of them were beautiful, and awfully sad. And some I couldn't understand.

Well, other people moved away. Carol and Vince moved, Vince kissed me good-by, and Carol gave me a lipstick that she said was the wrong color for her. And I took some of my money and bought her some eye shadow. I knew that was what she wanted. We said we'd write to each other and visit each other. But so far we haven't.

Mrs. Keating, the woman with the three boys and the married daughter, couldn't find a place for a long time. Then her oldest son got married, and the next one went in the Army, and Freddie got in trouble. Somebody caught him unscrewing a lock, and they asked him where he got the tools and he said Pop gave them to him, which was true. Only they didn't believe him. Anyway, he got sent away to school. And Mrs. Keating moved to her daughter's.

The crippled girl, her father died, and her mother couldn't manage things, so the girl had to go to a home. I hope it's a place where she can get books to read.

Pop found another job and we moved too. It's not as bad as I thought it would be. But it's not like the Almont, with its big rooms and windows. It's not near the river or the park.

The day before we moved, Mama and I were in the hall and Mr. Berger came down, and Mama said to him, Mr. Berger, I want to thank you for what you tried to do. I don't think we appreciated it enough.

He said, Oh, I didn't really do anything. I just think people should know what their rights are. Actually, if it hadn't been for Linda I wouldn't have cared to do anything.

And he shook hands with me and with Mama, and said, I hope you have a good place to go.

Mama said, It's not bad. And we wish you luck.

At last the day came for moving. We were all packed up and waiting for the truck. Nearly everybody was gone from the building, and a man was coming in from next door to take care of the ones that were left. It was summer, nearly a year since we moved in. I was stand-ing out in front when the mailman came by. He had a few letters, and one was for me.

When I saw the handwriting I almost flipped. It was from Sharon. I thought, Imagine if we had moved yesterday, I never would have gotten it. I tore it open. It said: Dear Linda, I'm coming home for a few days, and I'll be in the apartment till Daddy and I go off on a trip. I hope I'll see you. Maybe we can play a little tennis. Love, Sharon.

I didn't know what to do. We were leaving. But I *couldn't* leave without seeing her.

I ran in and said, Mama, Sharon's coming home! She'll be here tomorrow.

Mama was busy packing up the stuff from the refrigerator. She said, What? Don't bother me now, Linda, I'm busy.

I said, Mama, please listen to me, Sharon's coming home, what shall I do?

She said, You can't do anything. We're leaving as soon as the truck comes, don't I have enough trouble without you bothering me?

I ran out of the house thinking, I've got to get a message to her. She'll come here and nobody will be here.

Suddenly I had an idea. I ran down the street to her house. I thought, Let the truck come, they can go without me if they want. I don't care.

I went up in the elevator and rang the bell. I heard footsteps. The door opened and it was that same housekeeper.

I said, I'm Sharon's friend, and I had a letter from her. She's coming home and wants to see me, but I won't be there, so would you tell her I'll phone her?

100

The woman said, I don't know if you'll get her. Her father is planning to leave as soon as she gets here.

I said, Well, when will that be?

She said, I really don't know.

She wasn't trying to be too helpful.

I said, Well, could I give you my new address for her?

She told me to come in and write it down, so I did. I looked around while she was getting a pencil. It looked different. All her mother's pictures were gone from the walls. The furniture was the same but it was in different places.

I wrote: Dear Sharon, we're moving. The Almont is sold and is going to be torn down. I meant to write to you but I couldn't. Here is my new address. Please write me, and I'll phone you when you come back from your trip. All my love, Linda.

P.S. I have some wonderful stories to tell you.

Then I said good-by and ran home.

The truck was there and Pop and Joe were loading it. We were taking the sofa but not the dining room table because there wouldn't be room for it. We were only going to have three rooms, but it wouldn't matter because Joe would not be there. He was going in the Army. Mama felt pretty bad about that. She said he should be going to college, but Joe said maybe he'd take courses in the Army. Mama said lots of boys not half as bright as Joe were in college just because they had money.

So we moved. I waited to hear from Sharon, and while I was waiting, I wrote down all the stuff about the Almont that I could remember, to tell her. That's how this came to be written. It was a good building, and it's a shame it had to be demolished.

Once I went past that corner on the bus. I thought I would see a big apartment house with gold towers. But all I saw was a supermarket, a wide flat building with people pushing shopping carts.

I thought, So that's what they made us move for, and that's why they took away the Almont with its two stone lions. All that trouble for nothing.

Still, it wasn't just for nothing. Because there was a time when we had friends there, and had fun. We had trouble too, but we lived through it. I guess that's something. And I learned a few things. I learned to play tennis, and to turn the knife blades in when you set the table.

And I have this guitar. I couldn't look at it for a while. I had to tell Pop how I got it, and he didn't say much but the way he looked at me, I wouldn't want that to happen again. But now I'm playing pretty well. And when I play it I think of Miss Clark and wonder where she is. She didn't want an awful lot, but she didn't even get that. I wonder if she remembers me.

ABOUT THE AUTHOR: Eleanor Clymer spent her growing-up years in New York City. She attended Columbia and Bank Street College and New York University and graduated from the University of Wisconsin. Although Mrs. Clymer now lives in Katonah, New York, in the hills of northern Westchester County, she feels that city and country children are alike in many ways.

ABOUT THE ARTIST: David K. Stone lives in Port Washington, New York, with his wife and two children. His thirteen-year-old daughter, Kelly, says Mr. Stone, "shares many of the reactions Linda expresses in the story. Kelly became my valuable assistant by recommending clothing and hair styles. She also picked out the best idea for the jacket—two girls sitting and talking, which is something thirteen-year-olds do a lot of." Mr. Stone used charcoal on smooth illustration board for his drawings.

ABOUT THE BOOK: The title is set in Bulmer italic and the chapter numbers in Times Roman; the text type is Janson. The book is printed by offset.